CW0092123J

# Rosie Suter

# My Bedroom Window

Nightingale Books

NIGHTINGALE PAPERBACK

A CIP catalogue record for this title is
available from the British Library.
ISBN 978-1-83875-556-0

Nightingale Books is an imprint of
Pegasus Elliot MacKenzie Publishers Ltd.
www.pegasuspublishers.com

First Published in 2023

Nightingale Books
Sheraton House Castle Park
Cambridge England

Printed & Bound in Great Britain

## Dedication

I dedicate this book to
Teddy, Piper, Olivia, Evangeline, Evelyn, Non and Maya.

When I look out of my bedroom window
I can see…
…down into my back garden.

Sometimes I see a little grey squirrel
looking for food on the grass.

He always scampers away up a tree
if he sees me.

Maybe he thinks I might hurt him, but
I would only like to be his friend.

"Shshsh, Joe, keep very still," says Mummy.

But the little grey squirrel always disappears
as fast as he comes.

When I look out of my bedroom window
sometimes I see…
…a magpie standing high and proud.

He even dares to strut around the grass
when my kittens are not too far away.

He doesn't fly away until he has found
some scraps of bread or food left out
by my mummy or daddy.

"Shoo," says Daddy.

He says the magpies are not very kind birds
because they disturb the little birds' nests.

I don't think my kittens will bother him, and
he knows it. He is too bold and majestic.

When I look out of my bedroom window
sometimes I see…
….my two kittens walking along the garden wall
or stretching out in a shady spot under the bushes.

They are called Isabella and Charlie.

They are always pleased to see me,
even though I tug at their fur sometimes
when I am playing with them.

I don't mean to hurt them. I am just
cuddling them.

"Gently, Joe," say Mummy and Daddy.

When I look out of my bedroom window
sometimes I see…
…the man who lives at the house at the back of my garden,
cutting his grass with a lawn mower.

I can just see him over the fence.
I wish I could have a go.

He goes forwards and backwards,
backwards and forwards.

The machine makes a whirring, scraping noise.
Sometimes it goes quiet, then it starts all over again.

It takes a long time for him to finish the job.

"One day you can help me cut the grass, Joe,"
says Daddy. "When you are bigger."

When I look out of my bedroom window
sometimes I see…
…my Mummy hanging out some washing on the clothes line,
so that it can dry in the sunshine.

Then I rush down to be her helper.

She lets me hand her the pegs one at a time.
"You are a big help, Joe," she says.

Sometimes if it starts to rain, Mummy has to
quickly take everything indoors again.

She doesn't ask me to help her when that happens.

"Quick, quick, Joe. Run indoors and stay dry," she says.

When I look out of my bedroom window
sometimes all is still.

But if I listen very carefully…
…I can hear distant noises.

Sometimes I can hear the sound of a train
from a long way away.

It is like a rumbling noise. I can't see it,
because there are a lot of houses in the way,
but I know it is there.

I want to stand on my window sill to see better,
but Mummy says crossly, "That is dangerous, Joe.
You mustn't climb up! Stay on your chair,
if you want to look out of the window."

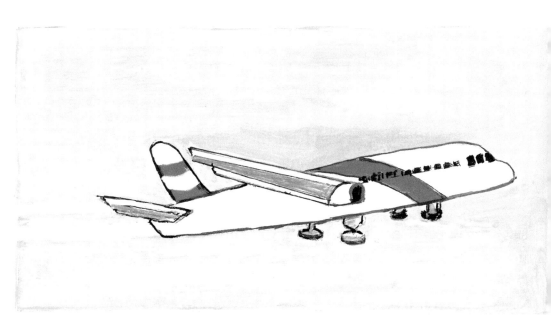

More often I hear the sound of an aeroplane
in the sky.

"Aeroplane, Joe!" says Daddy.

And he lifts me up and we go to the window.

I can usually see the aeroplane in the sky
a long way away.

Sometimes it leaves a little smoky pattern
behind it.

"I wonder where that aeroplane is off to,"
says Daddy dreamily.

It is very peaceful in my garden…

…even with the squirrels and magpies,
even with my two lazy kittens and
Mummy busily hanging out the clothes.

"I think I'll go downstairs now, and
play in the garden on my new bike
which makes the sound of a motor bike."

It makes a **B BRRM**, **B BRRM** noise.

"Charlie, Isabella," I call. "I'm coming
outside to play with you now.
Shall we look for squirrels and magpies?"

Then I hear a flutter of wings and
a scratching of little paws <sup>up</sup> and <sup>over</sup> the fence.

Can **YOU** see who they were?

What can **YOU** see out of your bedroom window?

## About the Author

Rosie Suter is a lover of the local community and believes each person has the ability to make a positive impact, by their words and deeds, to the person or landscape in front of them.

Although an accountant by profession, Rosie's heart is in the arts. Writing, reading, painting and photography fill her time, when she is not creating adventures with her grandchildren.

She has been a Sunday School worker for twenty years, and also helped at her youngest son's primary school in the book reading sessions.